HUGO the HARE'S Rainy Day

Jez Alborough

DOUBLEDAY

To Lucas

♪ *Hugo the Hare's Rainy Day Song* can be heard and downloaded, along with the sheet music, from **jezalborough.com/hugothehare**

HUGO THE HARE'S RAINY DAY
A DOUBLEDAY BOOK
978 0 857 53039 4

Published in Great Britain by Doubleday, an imprint of Random House Children's Publishers UK
A Random House Group Company

This edition published 2014

1 3 5 7 9 10 8 6 4 2

Copyright © Jez Alborough, 2014
Hugo the Hare's Rainy Day Song © Jez Alborough, 2014

With thanks to Philippa and Dave for help with the musical notation.

RANDOM HOUSE CHILDREN'S PUBLISHERS UK
61–63 Uxbridge Road, London W5 5SA

www.**randomhousechildrens**.co.uk
www.**randomhouse**.co.uk

Addresses for companies within The Random House Group Limited can be found at:
www.randomhouse.co.uk/offices.htm

THE RANDOM HOUSE GROUP Limited Reg. No. 954009

A CIP catalogue record for this book is available from the British Library.

Printed in China

FSC
www.fsc.org

MIX
Paper from
responsible sources
FSC® C104723

The Random House Group Limited supports the Forest Stewardship Council® (FSC®),
the leading international forest certification organisation. Our books carrying the FSC label are printed on
FSC®-certified paper. FSC is the only forest certification scheme supported by the leading environmental organisations,
including Greenpeace. Our paper procurement policy can be found at www.randomhouse.co.uk/environment.

Weather +
Seasons

Hugo the Hare came out one day
to go to the park with his friends to play.
He sniffed at the air and said, 'I can smell wet,
and wet is one thing that I don't like to get.'

Billy the Goat had a smile on his face,
he was kicking a ball round to Hugo's place.

'Why are you carrying that?' Billy said,
when he saw the umbrella above Hugo's head.

'Because,' said Hugo, 'it's going to get wet
and wet is one thing that I don't like to get.'
'No it's not,' said Billy, 'just look at the sky,
the sun is shining, it's warm and it's dry.'

They talked and they walked and it didn't take long
for one drip of rain to prove Billy wrong.
Billy just shrugged. 'It's only a drop,
I'm not bothered,' he said, 'it will probably stop.'

But it **PLOPPED**, it **PLIPPED** and it **PLOPPED** some more. And before very long it started to pour.

It fell on the path with a **PITTER-PAT-PAT**.
It bounced off the brolly with a **RAT-A-TAT-TAT**.
It **SPLATTERED** on Billy from high in the sky,
he got wetter and wetter, while Hugo stayed dry.

Hugo felt bad
because inside he knew
what a good little hare
would probably do.
His head didn't want to
but his heart said he should
and he knew his friend Billy
was hoping he would.

So he said,
'You're getting all wet, I can see . . .
would you like to share
my umbrella with me?'
'Oh thank you,' said Billy.
'I really don't mind
but I'd better say "yes"
as you're being so kind.'

So under the brolly they shuffled along
until Hugo noticed that something was wrong.

'Billy, you're pushing me out,' Hugo cried.
'My fur – it's getting all wet down one side.'
Billy looked over, he could see it was true,
Hugo's umbrella was not built for two.

'Squeeze closer,' he said – they tried once again,
but then Billy's shoulder stuck out in the rain.

'Hugo,' he said, 'I've just had an idea,
the umbrella's too small so the answer is clear.
If we want to fit two of us snugly inside
then we need to make both of our bodies less wide.'

'But how?' wondered Hugo, not following at all.

'It's easy,' said Billy, 'we make ourselves tall.'

He sat on a log by the side of the track,

'Now, Hugo,' he ordered, 'hop up on my back.'

'All right,' said Hugo, though the plan sounded silly,
he ran and he hopped . . . and he landed on Billy.

'Now, climb up,' said Billy, 'and then we'll be tall

and
out of
the place
where the
raindrops
can fall.'

Billy shuffled along with Hugo on top
and though the rain fell they felt not a drop.

Then, off in the distance, Hugo could see
Nat the Cat sheltering under a tree.

'What are you doing up there?' she cried.
'Keeping dry,' said Hugo, 'by being less wide,
but I'd rather keep dry standing under your tree.'
'Come on down,' said Nat, 'you can stand beside me.'

There was only one problem
that Nat could see –
a great big wet puddle
between them and the tree.
Billy dug in his hooves
to get a good grip
he teetered and tottered
and tried not to slip.

'Come on,' cried Nat,
'there's not far to go.'
But that was before
the wind started to blow.
It blasted the brolly
with all of its might
and pulled Hugo Hare
to the left, then the right.

'*The umbrella!*' cried Billy,
as they started to sway.
'Let go of it *now*
or you'll get blown away.'

'But I need it,' cried Hugo,
'we're not there yet –
**I TOLD YOU
BEFORE . . .**

I DON'T LIKE
TO GET WET!'

But the wind didn't care
as upwards it blew,
it lifted the brolly and Hugo Hare too.
He flew through the air and like it or not . . .

SPLASH!

Wet was exactly what Hugo Hare got.

Nat saw that Hugo was really upset,
everyone knows that he hates to get wet.
But Nat also knew things could only get better –
if you're already wet you can't get any wetter.

So out from under the branches Nat came,
yelling, 'I want to play the getting-wet game.'
She skipped to the puddle where Hugo had crashed,
then into the water she **SPLISHED** and she **SPLASHED**.

Then Billy Goat smiled and cried, 'Wait for me.'
He **SPLOSHED** in the water and that made three.

They **SLAPPED** and **SLOPPED** in the slippery wet
each getting the wettest of wet they could get.

They stayed and they played in the puddle until
suddenly something made Hugo stand still.
The water no longer **PLIPPITY-PLOPPED**.
'Look up,' he cried, 'the rain has stopped.'

The clouds had all disappeared from the sky,
now it was time to get themselves dry.
As they sat in the sun Nat made up a song
and both of her friends started singing along.

But when Hu-go played the get-ting wet game, he for-

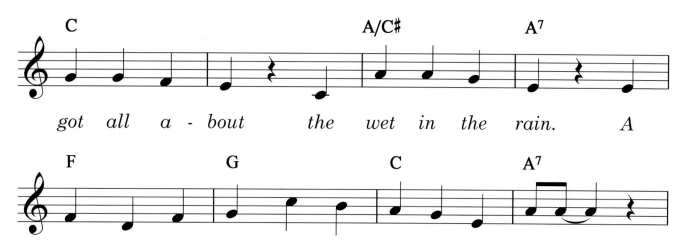

got all a-bout the wet in the rain. A

SPLISH and a SPLASH he be-gan to feel bet-ter.

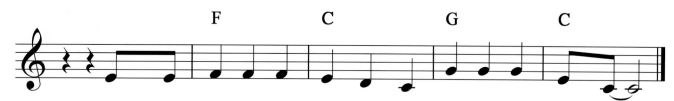

When you're al-rea-dy wet you can't get a-ny wet-ter.

They played with the ball for a while, and by then
all the three friends were dry once again.
But each of them knew they would never forget
the wonderful day Hugo got himself wet.